To my son Marco - ISC

Created exclusively for World International Limited by Bloomsbury Publishing Plc
First published in Great Britain in 1997 by World International Limited, Deanway
Technology Centre, Wilmslow Road, Handforth, Cheshire SK9 3FB

Copyright © Text Mary Hooper 1997
Copyright © Illustrations Ivana Svabic-Cannon 1997
Art Direction Lisa Coombes

The moral right of the author and illustrator has been asserted
A CIP catalogue record of this book is available from the
British Library

ISBN 0 7498 3088 3

Printed by Bath Press, Great Britain

10 9 8 7 6 5 4 3 2 1

Little Readers

FREDDIE the FIBBER

Mary Hooper

Pictures by Ivana Svabic-Cannon

World International Limited

Freddie was a dear little boy. A bright-eyed, shiny-haired, nice little boy.

But . . . Freddie told *fibs*. Dreadful, walloping, warthog-sized fibs. He just couldn't seem to stop himself. And this is what happened to him . . .

One morning, he came down the stairs like this:

"Go and get dressed properly," Mummy said. "I like you in your new shirt. Go and put that on."

"It's gone!" said Freddie. (He hated his new shirt, and had stuffed it behind the wardrobe.) "A fox got it! A fox ran in, picked up my shirt in his teeth, and ran out!"

"Oh Freddie, you are a *fibber*!" Mummy said, and sighed.

At lunchtime, Freddie was starving. He was
so hungry that he ate his own sandwich in seconds –
and then he ate his baby sister's sandwich, too.

"What on **earth's** going on?" Mummy cried.

"It was a bear!" said Freddie. "A great grizzly bear!
It came in here, snatched our sandwiches, and ate
them in one gulp!"

"Oh Freddie!" Mummy said crossly. "You and your *fibs*!"
And she sent Freddie outside.

Freddie played football in the garden.

He tackled the ball and squashed all the daffodils.

"Oh Freddie!" Mummy shrieked.

"Look what you've done!"

"It wasn't **me!**" said Freddie. "It was a herd of elephants.
They stampeded right through the flowerbeds!"
Freddie's mummy groaned. She sent Freddie inside.

In the sitting room, Freddie eyed the box of chocolates
that Mummy had got for her birthday. Mummy was
letting Freddie eat one chocolate each day.
But that wasn't enough for Freddie.
He wanted more chocolates, and he wanted them NOW!

So he had his
today's chocolate.

And he had tomorrow's
chocolate.

And the next day's.

Soon he was up to
Friday fortnight.

And by the time he was up to
Christmas, the box was empty.

"Oh Freddie!" Mummy cried. "NOW what have you done? Where are all those chocolates?"

"The Greater-Spotted-Choccy-Eater crawled in, put his snout under the lid, and gobbled them all up!"

"This is too much!" Mummy shouted.
And she sent Freddie upstairs.

This was a mistake. Freddie's room looked like a pig sty.

"Oh Freddie!" Mummy wailed when she came up. "What have you been doing in here?"

"Just playing quietly," said Freddie.

"But then a posse of cowboys rode in and started
whooping about the place. They made a terrible mess."
"Oh Freddie! Freddie!" Mummy cried. And she sent
Freddie downstairs.

Freddie went to play with his friend next door – just for half an hour, Mummy said.

But Freddie forgot the time. Well, he didn't actually forget, he just couldn't be bothered to worry about it.

And he had a very good excuse for getting home late, a fabo-fib, a super-porky.

"Freddie!" Mummy said, when he got in. "What time do you call this?!"

"Sorry," Freddie said, "but you'll never guess what happened! You see, we were riding our bikes round and round the garden, and a big spaceship came down and green aliens got out and pointed their ray-beams at us and captured us and . . ."

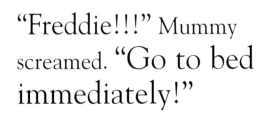

"Freddie!!!" Mummy screamed. "Go to bed immediately!"

Freddie didn't stop to make up any more fibs. He knew when enough was enough.

That night, Freddie had a very scary dream . . .

He was just putting on his best shirt, when a fox ran into his bedroom, ripped off the shirt with its sharp teeth, and ran out with it.

He was just about to tuck into a tasty sandwich, when a great grizzly bear tore the door off its hinges, and almost bit Freddie's hand off as it gobbled up the sandwich.

He was just recovering
from this when a herd of
elephants stampeded right
through his room.

And he'd just picked himself up and was reaching out for one of Mummy's chocolates when a great spotty monster came through the window and gulped them down, box and all.

Then a posse of cowboys
charged through the walls,
trampling on his toys and
flattening all the furniture.

"Oh help!" Freddie yelled
into the darkness. "What's
happening?"

Suddenly a great ladder appeared out of the sky and
down came green aliens. They pointed their ray-
beams at him.

"Mummeeee!" Freddie screamed, waking up in a
terrible fright.

"Mummeeee! Save me!"

Mummy rushed into Freddie's room.

"Whatever is it, Freddie?"

"It was horrible . . . horrible . . . " Freddie said in a wobbly voice. "First there was a fierce fox, then a great grizzly bear, then a herd of elephants, then a huge spotty monster and then a posse of cowboys who knocked all my bedroom down so that nasty green aliens could come and get me!"

"Oh, Freddie," said Mummy. "I'm so tired of all your *fibs*. Why do you keep telling these stories? What do you want?"

"I want a cuddle!" said poor Freddie, and he burst into tears.

"I'm not going to tell any
more *fibs*, Mummy. Not ever."

Do you believe him?